Invitation to be THANKFUL

You're Invited!

Written by:

JULIE SPIVEY

Illustrated by: Windel Eborlas

To order additional copies of this book, contact:
Xlibris
844-714-8691
www.Xlibris.com
Orders@Xlibris.com

ISBN: 978-1-6641-5883-2 (sc)
ISBN: 978-1-6641-5884-9 (hc)
ISBN: 978-1-6641-5882-5 (e)

Print information available on the last page

Rev. date: 03/02/2021

Invitation to be
THANKFUL

YOU'RE INVITED!!

Who's Invited? **YOU!**

What's the event? **A Thankfulness Celebration**

When? **Let's start NOW!**

Why? **Because being thankful will actually make you feel better. You will be happier and healthier!**

Where? **This thankfulness celebration can happen wherever YOU are RIGHT NOW and wherever you CHOOSE to take it in your future!**

Let's get this party started!

Wait! A thankfulness celebration? Maybe you're thinking...

Don't we already have a day that we call Thanksgiving?

True, we DO have a day set aside each year that we call Thanksgiving... it's a day to gather with family and friends as we reflect and give thanks.

What, exactly, does it mean to be thankful?
What does it LOOK like and SOUND
like to have a grateful heart?

Let's *compare* the same 5 situations...
a negative, ungrateful attitude

VS

a positive, grateful attitude.

Being a thankful person takes practice. Yep, practice! Think of tossing a ball or riding a bike...the first time you tried, it probably wasn't very good, right?

It's the same with being thankful. The more you do it, the easier & more natural it becomes. Eventually, having a grateful heart becomes a part of who you are as a person.

So...HOW do you "practice" thankfulness, you ask? Here are a few ideas to start with...

- Simply say "thank you" every chance you get!

- Set aside time each day to record things in a "gratitude journal." For example, every night before going to bed, write 5 things that you are thankful for...big things and little things!

- Share your thankful list daily (or weekly) with a close friend or family member. Accountability really helps!

- Hang a poster up in your bedroom or your classroom & add to it every day.

- Use a dry erase marker & write things you're grateful for on your bathroom mirror.

- Write thank you notes often to people in your life that you are grateful for—tell them why you're thankful for them.

When you develop a healthy habit of having thankful thoughts, you'll discover that you actually start LOOKING for things to be thankful for as you go about your day. This creates positivity in your day!

Maybe "the old you" would have found something to complain about, but the "new you" expresses gratitude instead. Thankfulness becomes more natural & rooted within you. You'll find that you are much happier this way.

When you choose to be a thankful person, others will ENJOY being around you more. Your positivity & grateful heart will likely spread to others!

Thankfulness is CONTAGIOUS!!

So, just as with an invitation to a
birthday party, you have a
CHOICE to either GO to the party
or NOT GO to the party.

Thankfulness is a choice too! When you
accept the invitation to be thankful, then you
are making a CHOICE to "look on the bright
side" of your situations...CHOOSE to find
something good in everyone & everything.

There is
ALWAYS, ALWAYS, ALWAYS

something
to be thankful for!!

Let's start now!! ☺
The next few pages have been left blank for you...
I encourage you to jot down ALL the things you
are thankful for & invite others to do the same!
Cover every square inch of the page with every
little thing that comes to mind that you are
thankful for - nothing is too big or too small!

Printed in the United States
By Bookmasters